A Balloon for Grandad

ORCHARD BOOKS
338 Euston Road, London NW1 3BH
Orchard Books Australia
17/207 Kent Street, Sydney NSW 2000
ISBN 978 184362 102 7
First published by Orchard Books in 1988
First paperback publication in 1994
This edition published in 2002
Text © Nigel Gray 1988
Illustrations © Jane Ray 1988

A CIP catalogue record for this book is available from the British Library.
3 5 7 9 10 8 6 4
Printed in China
Orchard Books is a division of Hachette Children's Books,
an Hachette UK company.
www.hachette.co.uk

A Balloon for Grandad

Nigel Gray

pictures by Jane Ray

ORCHARD BOOKS

For Sam and Grandad Abdulla

N.G.

For David

J.R.

It was a warm day
so the back door stood wide open.
Sam's balloon
snuggled up against the ceiling.
It was bobbing and bumping in the breeze.

 After breakfast,
Sam and Dad
went upstairs to wash their hands.

Then from the bathroom window
Dad caught sight
of a glint of silver and red.
"Look! There goes your balloon," he said.
"It must have blown out of the back door!"

 They watched it rising up
as straight and smooth as an elevator
on its way to the very top floor
of a building taller
than the tallest tree.

They ran downstairs and went outside.
Up and up went the balloon,
jerkily, fidgety now, in fits and starts
like a rock climber
zig-zagging up a cliff.

And then,
when it was so high
it looked like a tiny red berry in the sky,
the wind grabbed it.
"I want my balloon," Sam cried.

"No!" said the wind. "It's mine!
All mine!"
And off rushed the balloon,
in a hurry now,
south, towards the mountains.

"Don't cry," said Dad.
"Across the mountains is the sea,
and across the sea is the desert,
and across the desert, a river,
and in the river, an island."

"And on that island," said Sam,
"my grandad Abdulla lives
looking after his goats
and tending his date trees."

"That's right," said Dad.

"Perhaps," said Sam,
"my balloon
is going to visit Grandad Abdulla."

"Yes," said Dad.
"Then it will fly
high, high, high
over the snow-decorated mountains
where golden eagles nest;

high, high over the sparkling
blue-green sea where silver fish
leap from the waves;

high over the hot yellow sand
of the desert
where scorpions,
and spitting spiders,
and sidewinder snakes
hide from the heat."

"And sandgrouse will peck at it," said Sam,
"and falcons will fall on it,
and hawks will fly after it,
and vultures with their big hooky beaks
and their sharp talons will tear at it,

but the dry desert wind
will help it to dodge and weave
and nothing will harm it.''

"That's right," said Dad.
"And then,
tired after its long journey,
it will see down below
the long blue ribbon of the river;

it will see the small
gold and emerald jewel
of the island;
it will see the little brown house
built of baked mud.''

"Yes," said Sam,
"and it will see Grandad Abdulla
sitting in the shade of his mango tree.
And down, down, down it will glide,
landing in the yard
like a seagull settling on the sea.

 And Grandad Abdulla will say,
'A balloon!
A balloon for me!
My grandson Sam must have sent it
to show that,
although he's so far away,
he's thinking of me.' "

"Yes. It's sad to see it go," said Dad,
"but the balloon will be happy
after its great adventure.

And Grandad Abdulla will be happy
thinking of you."

 "I'm glad my balloon's
gone to see Grandad," said Sam,
"because if I know Grandad's happy,
then I feel happy too."